No Shoes

CAROLYN BRYANT
Illustrations by VICTOR GUIZA

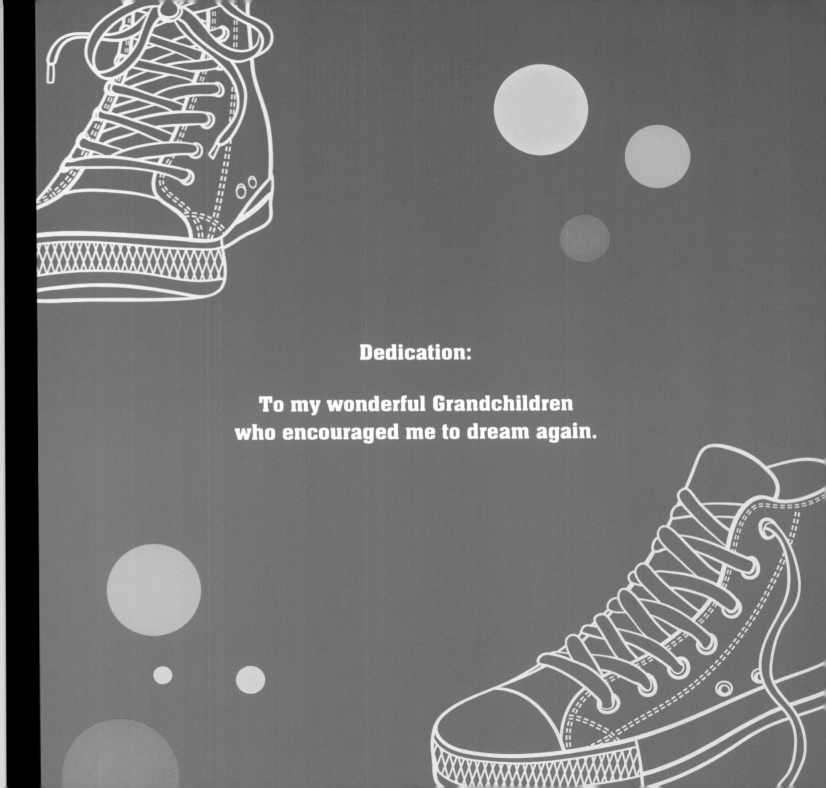

Dedication:

To my wonderful Grandchildren
who encouraged me to dream again.

One afternoon, Jamison woke up from a dream after taking a long nap. He looked at his dog Maxx, who is a terrier poodle.

"Maxx," said Jamison. "I had a dream that I had no shoes on." At that moment Maxx went and picked up a brand-new pair of shoes off the floor, as if he understood what Jamison was saying.

Jamison looked surprised!

"I guess it was not a dream after all!" Jamison said with excitement.

"**Now** I remember," said Jamison. "It wasn't a dream at all!"

"I remember I was so hungry that I ran out the door to get some food."

"I live next to Main Street—they have a lot of restaurants and stores."

So Jamison came up to Bert and Bob's Bakery; they have a lot of sweet-smelling foods. "I like her sweet-potato pie a lot," said Jamison.

As soon as Jamison walked in the store, people looked at him with surprise and said, "You have no shoes on, you can't come in here."

Jamison ran out the door and his feelings were hurt. But Jamison was still hungry, so he walked further down the street.

So he came up to Busterbrown Burgers—best burgers around town. Jamison's mouth started to water as he thought about the Buster Burger. It has a turkey burger with bacon, cheese, pineapple, and avocado, and chili fries on a Hawaiian bun with a glass of cold water. Um Um!

As soon as Jamison walked in the store, people looked at him with surprise and said, "You have no shoes on, you can't come in here."

Jamison had tears in his eyes! "Just because I forgot my shoes," said Jamison, "now I can't get any food to eat."

Just as Jamison started walking back home, a boy coming out of the store with his dad stopped Jamison. "Wait a minute," he said, "you can have my new pair of shoes and my burger and fries." The boy's dad said it was okay.

Jamison was so excited! He said, "Thank you, thank you!"

Jamison put the shoes on and sat on the bench by the store and ate his food.

Jamison ran home and told his mother what had happened. His mother said, "The boy had compassion for you."

"What is 'compassion'?" Jamison asked. "Showing kindness and care for another!" replied his mother.

"Oh!" said Jamison. Jamison's mother said, "Remember how someone showed compassion to you, and make sure to pass it on."

"**Jamison,** wait a minute—how did you forget your shoes?"

God gave us examples though Jesus Christ how to have compassion for others:

Now Jesus called His disciples to Himself and said, "I have compassion on the multitude, because they have now continued with me three days and have nothing to eat. And I do not want to send them away hungry, lest they faint on the way." Matthew 15:32 NKJV

CPSIA information can be obtained
at www.ICGtesting.com
Printed in the USA
BVHW020551211120
593553BV00002B/27